Trusting God

By Terry Phillips Griffin

Editor: Michelle "Mike" Hileman

Trusting God Copyright 2025 by Terry Phillips Griffin

Case ID 1-15038363551

www.terrypgriffin.com

Trusting God

By Terry Phillips Griffin

In October 2020, Mary Jo Silzell taught us a great deal about trusting our Sovereign God as she shared her incredible testimony during our Grand Lake Adventure at the Raders' Lakehouse.

Mary Jo says, "It is good simply because God chose it for you. So, hang on and enjoy the ride!" She wholeheartedly embraces this conviction in her life. I am honored and privileged to dedicate this book to Mary Jo for her teachings. My wonderful friends and I from Red River Cowboy Church will be forever grateful!

1

Chapter One

We understand the meaning of the word "trust" because we have people we know we can rely on. We trust and believe they will help us when we need them.

Over time, we develop a close relationship with them that is built on trust.

Building a close relationship with a family member or friend requires time. As you deepen your understanding of God and His immense love for you, you also begin to recognize that you can trust Him!

3

Chapter One - Trusting God

Consider the beautiful creations around you. I'm sure you've noticed how stunning the sky looks on a clear day, with fluffy white clouds drifting lazily by. You know how bright and colorful a flower with delicate petals and tiny leaves can appear.

We can hear birds chirping and watch their small wings carry them swiftly from tree to tree. These wonders are just a small part of God's glorious creation, made in the beginning.

These creations did not merely evolve over millions of years, as some suggest; they were completely brought into existence during the six days of creation-spoken into being by our powerful Creator God!

Chapter Two

We can trust God because He is Who He says He is! The Bible describes God as the great "**I AM.**" It also offers insights into God's character and attributes.

We can use three words to uniquely describe our Creator God. The first word is Omnipotent, which means All-Powerful.

God is so powerful that He **SPOKE** the universe into existence. No other power in heaven or on earth can compare with the creative power of our One True God.

Chapter Two - Trusting God

The Bible explains that God's power holds everything together and in place! His power is the reason we experience daylight and darkness every 24 hours as the Earth rotates and orbits the sun, much like the hands of a clock move steadily and continuously around its face.

The world was created and positioned in the heavens at a specific distance from the sun, ensuring that it does not burn or freeze us to death.

God holds all things **IN PLACE** and in an orderly fashion because **HE IS** the All-Powerful **GOD**.

 **Omnipotent** *means that God is all-powerful.*

Chapter Two - Trusting God

The second word to describe God is Omniscient, which means God is all-knowing. God knows everything! No other intelligence, including artificial intelligence, can compare to our great God.

He knows the beginning from the end because He had no beginning or ending. God is eternal. He has always existed, and He will always exist.

Those who claim otherwise have been deceived. They have been misled by the same enemy (Satan) who deceived Adam and Eve in the garden of Eden at the very beginning of creation.

 **Omniscient** means that God knows all.

8

Chapter Two - Trusting God

The third word is Omnipresent. This term means that God is everywhere at the same time. Our great and true God is the only Being who can be present everywhere in the universe-all at once!

Some people have used the three "omni" words to describe a fictional character in a book. But Omnipotent, Omniscient, and Omnipresent are true only of our One great God who created the heavens, the earth, and every living being.

Omnipresent means that God is everywhere.

Chapter Three

We can trust God because of His character! The character of God means all the things about Him that make Him GOD! Here are some attributes of God's character:

GOD is ETERNAL

God always has been, and He always will be. God never changes. (Psalm 90:2)

GOD is SOVEREIGN

God alone is in control of everything. He has a plan for His people and will carry out His plan! God does as He wishes. (Isaiah 46:9b-10 and Psalm 115:3)

Chapter Three - Trusting God

Psalm 90:2 (NKJV)

"Before the mountains were brought forth, Or ever You had formed the earth and the world, Even from everlasting to everlasting, You are God."

Isaiah 46:9b-10 (NKJV)

"For I am God, and there is no other; I am God, and there is none like Me, Declaring the end from the beginning, And from ancient times things that are not yet done, Saying, "My counsel shall stand, And I will do all My pleasure,"

Psalm 115:3 (NKJV)

"But our God is in heaven; He does whatever He pleases."

Chapter Three - Trusting God

GOD is HOLY.

God cannot sin, and He hates all sin. God is wholly set apart from the rest of His creation because He has never sinned. If God sinned, He would not be **GOD**. He alone is entirely **HOLY**. (1 Samuel 2:2)

GOD is JUST.

God is just, meaning He is fair. Because He is just, He must punish sin. The Bible tells us He is coming to judge the earth with truth. (Psalm 96:12-13)

GOD is FAITHFUL.

God **ALWAYS** keeps His promises. He does not lie. (Numbers 23:19)

Chapter Three - Trusting God

1 Samuel 2:2 (CSB)

There is no one holy like the Lord. There is no one besides you! And there is no rock like our God.

Psalm 96:12-13 (CSB)

Let the field and everything in it exult. Then all the trees of the forest will shout for joy before the Lord, for he is coming-for he is coming to judge the earth. He will judge the world with righteousness and the peoples with his faithfulness.

Numbers 23:19 (CSB)

God is not a man, that he might lie, or a son of man, that he might change his mind.

Chapter Three - Trusting God

GOD is FORGIVING.

God will always forgive us when we ask Him to. (1 John 1:9)

GOD is RIGHTEOUS.

As believers, we have been given a new nature because we are new people in Christ! We must live by God's standards found in the Bible. (Ephesians 4:22-24)

We cannot live by God's standards in our own strength. God gives everyone who trusts in Jesus as their Lord and Savior the gift of His Holy Spirit!

As believers in Jesus, the Holy Spirit of God now lives **IN US** to help us do the right things and make the right choices. The Holy Spirit reminds us that when we sin, we should ask for forgiveness immediately and then turn away from it! (repent)

1 John 1:19 (CSB)

If we confess our sins, he is faithful and righteous to forgive us our sins and to cleanse us from all unrighteousness.

Ephesians 4:22-24 (CSB)

To take off your former way of life, the old self that is corrupted by deceitful desires, to be renewed in the spirit of your minds, and to put on the new self, the one created according to God's likeness in righteousness and purity of the truth.

Chapter Three - Trusting God

Ephesians 1:7 (CSB)

In him we have redemption through his blood, the forgiveness of our trespasses, according to the riches of his grace.

John 14:16-17 (CSB)

And I will ask the Father, and he will give you another Counselor to be with you forever. He is the Spirit of truth. The world is unable to receive him because it doesn't see him or know him. But you do know him, because he remains with you and will be in you.

1 Thessalonians 5:15-18 (NLT)

See that no one pays back evil for evil, but always try to do good to each other and to all people. Always be joyful. Never stop praying. Be thankful in all circumstances, for this is God's will for you who belong to Christ Jesus.

18

Chapter Four

We can trust God because He has given us His Word.

GOD'S WORD is TRUTH.

We must believe what He says and live like we believe it.

Psalm 119:160 (CSB)

The entirety of your word is truth, each of your righteous judgments endures forever.

Proverbs 30:5 (CSB)

Every word of God is pure; he is a shield to those who take refuge in him.

21

Chapter Four - Trusting God

The words of Jesus recorded in the book of John chapter 14 verse 6 quote Jesus as saying, "I am the way, the truth, and the life. No one can come to the Father except through me."

GOD NEVER CHANGES.

Because God never changes, my future in heaven is secure! (Isaiah 41:4) Just imagine! The very Words of God are in the Holy Bible!

The Bible is a miraculous book, written by over 40 men over a span of approximately 1,500 to 1,600 years, with one continuous story theme: the redemption of humanity from a fallen and sin-filled world.

Chapter Four - Trusting God

There is no other book ever written that contains the words of God, inspired by God, and recorded by men in their own words. The Bible is the number one best-selling book because it is completely true and has the power to change people's lives!

The Bible tells us how everything began, how sin entered the world, and how God sent His Son into the world to die on the cross in order to save us from our sins.

We should be so thankful that Jesus gave up His life to save us. Because of our sinful nature, we could never be good enough to stand before our holy and righteous God on our own. We needed a Savior! We needed Jesus!

Chapter Four - Trusting God

The Bible is a history book that begins in Genesis and ends in Revelation, with the Kingdom of God breaking in and invading the kingdom of sin and darkness, as told in the story of God's Wonderful Plan. God came to rescue humanity and bring us into His Kingdom of Light! (Colossians 1:12-14)

At least one-third of the Bible consists of prophecy. The term prophecy refers to predicting or foretelling future events. All the Bible's prophecies that have already occurred have happened exactly as the prophets predicted. We are still waiting for the prophecies of the End Time to be fulfilled.

These prophets foretold the coming Messiah hundreds of years before Jesus was born.

Chapter Four - Trusting God

The prophecies concerning the return of the resurrected Jesus are the central event all believers look forward to. We refer to this as Jesus' Second Coming. Prophecy states that He will come back in the clouds, accompanied by heavenly angels and all believers who have already passed on to heaven.

We believe this will happen very soon! The Bible has instructed us to watch and wait for Jesus' Second Coming.

We know we can trust God about this because every prediction in the Bible has come true up to today. Therefore, we can be assured that those concerning Jesus' Second Coming will also come true.

Chapter Five

Understanding the A-B-Cs

The most important thing in life is understanding God's Plan to save us (redeem us) from our sins.

The Apostle Paul tells us what "the gospel" of salvation is. The word gospel means "good news."

It is the good news of Jesus Christ that saves us from eternal punishment and separation from God. Paul preached this gospel to the people of Corinth:

Christ died for our sins according to the scriptures, that He was buried, and that He rose again on the third day according to the scriptures. (1 Corinthians 15:4)

Chapter Five - Trusting God

Jesus is alive, and through Him, our sins can be forgiven. Our relationship with God can be restored.

It is important to remember that no one knows if today will be their last.

If you have not trusted God to save you, please read the A, B, Cs of Salvation below:

A - Admit you are a sinner. The Bible explains in Romans 3:23, **"For all have sinned and fall short of the glory of God."**

No one can keep God's Words perfectly 100% of the time. Admit you are a sinner and ask God to forgive you of your sins.

B - Believe in your heart. Believe that Jesus Christ died for your sins, was buried, and that God raised Him from the dead. This means trusting fully that Jesus IS who He says He is (the Son of God) and that He is the only Way you can be saved from the penalty of your sins. (John 3:16)

C - Call upon the name of the Lord. This means to trust in your heart and confess with your mouth that Jesus Christ is your Lord and Savior. You can then know that you are forgiven and will be safe forever in God's loving arms. (Romans 10:9-10)

The wisest choice you will ever make is to put your **TRUST in GOD** through His Son, Jesus!

Chapter Five - Trusting God

Dear God,

You are holy, and we are not-but through Jesus, You made a way for us to become holy too. Thank You for living in the hearts of all who believe and helping us grow to be more like Jesus each day.

You are Almighty-there is no one like You! You need nothing, yet You want a relationship with us. Thank You for being our good, good Father.

Thank You for giving us the Bible so we can know the truth when Satan tries to lie. Your Word is truth, and You never lie. Help us trust You and stand firm by learning Your Word and talking to You in prayer.

Thank You for Your love and protection.

In Jesus' Name, Amen.